for Max

First published in the United States in 1987
by E. P. Dutton, 2 Park Avenue, New York, N.Y. 10016

Originally published in Great Britain in 1986
by The Bodley Head Ltd, 30 Bedford Square, London WC1B 3RP

Printed in Great Britain by W. S. Cowell Ltd, Ipswich
ISBN: 0-525-44282-0   OBE   First Edition   10 9 8 7 6 5 4 3 2 1

The Perfect Day

John Prater

E. P. Dutton   New York

The Smiths are off to the beach for the day.

Soon everything is packed up, and everyone is ready to go.

Everyone, that is, except Kevin.

But at last they are on their way.

The sun shines and the birds sing.

They can't wait to get down to the beach.

It's a beautiful day, and there are lots of interesting places to explore.

I've got seaweed in my toes, and I almost stepped on a dead crab over there!

The sea is warm and calm.

At lunchtime they eat at a nice outdoor restaurant.

In the afternoon they go to the zoo, and arrive just in time to see the seals being fed.

Then they go to the amusement park by the beach.

Kevin and his sister ride on nearly everything

and they both win a prize.

But at the end of a perfect day, a sudden storm sends the family rushing for their car.